TOM FEELINGS

SOMETHING ON MY MIND

words by NIKKI GRIMES

DIAL BOOKS FOR YOUNG READERS · New York

Dial Books for Young Readers
A Division of E. P. Dutton
A Division of New American Library
2 Park Avenue New York, New York 10016

Published simultaneously in Canada
by Fitzhenry & Whiteside Limited, Toronto

Library of Congress Catalog Card Number: 77-86266
Printed in Hong Kong by South China Printing Co.
First Pied Piper Printing 1986
COBE
1 2 3 4 5 6 7 8 9 10

A Pied Piper Book is a registered trademark of
Dial Books for Young Readers,
a division of E. P. Dutton, a division of New American Library,
®TM 1,163,686 and ®TM 1,054,312

SOMETHING ON MY MIND
is published in a hardcover edition by
Dial Books for Young Readers.
ISBN 0-8037-0273-6

Illustrations for *Mama never understood* and *waiting*,
verses three and four, reprinted by
permission of Lothrop, Lee & Shepherd
from *Black Pilgrimage* by Tom Feelings.
Copyright ©1972 by Tom Feelings.

For my sons,
Kevin, Zamani, and Kamili.

TF

For Christ, who made it possible
and for Fola, who made it a challenge.

NG

Standing at the gate,
looking at the city,
home.
Talking make-believe.
Dee Dee say she's going down south one day,
visit her cousins.
But she won't pick no cotton. No.
Ronnie say never mind south.
He's going to Africa and live.
Frankie asked him if he could speak African.
Ronnie say jambo means hello
and he could learn the rest when he got there.
Frankie say she wants to go someplace that has no name.
Dee Dee say where is that?
She say where I could just be Frankie Lee,
and not have to feel worse than white people, or better,
and feel at home,
and happy,
and not always wishing I was someplace else.
Dee Dee and Ronnie say they want to go there too.

Seems I'm never old enough
to know the secrets
grown-ups share.
You wouldn't understand,
they say.
But when I'm wrong,
you hear them shout,
Girl, you should have known!

Sunday morning.
Me and Mama
off to church.
Smile pretty now.
Wear your nice dress,
we're going to visit the Lord's House,
she says,
then bangs her toe
and cusses.
I want to ask,
Instead of going to the Lord's house,
why don't we invite Him to visit ours?

I remember
wanting to be big like Mikey,
to stand around looking cool.
Now that I am,
it's OK I guess.
Some days I won't even smile
no matter what.
That's part of being cool.
The only thing is
I can't cry if I want to.

Outside.
I want to play,
to belong.
I want a friend to whisper to,
to keep my secrets
and to tell me hers.
I want to be
Inside.

little sister
holds on tight.
My hands hurt
from all that squeezing,
but I don't mind.
She thinks no one will bother her
when I'm around,
and they won't
if I can help it.
And even when I can't,
I try
'cause she believes in me.

Mama never understood
hanging in the park.
My brother Tommy said
it was being with friends
and not having to talk,
and looking at the boys play ball,
and wishing hard
that one of them was good enough
to be a star one day,
and feeling that
it didn't matter who.
What counted was that he could come back
and shine for us.

It don't matter
who people are
when we're together.
We got our own jokes
and they don't even know
when to laugh.

Waiting
for summer to end.
I've used up all the fun.
I wish school would start again
so there would be something to do.

Waiting
for someone to play with.
I'll be glad when I'm bigger.
Then I can go down the street
and play with the older kids
and won't have to sit here
alone.

Waiting
for lunchtime.
When it comes,
the school day will be
half over
and we can go
play doubledutch.

Waiting,
Daddy says,
is part of being a kid.
You wait to grow up
to leave school
to go to work
to live alone
always waiting.
I wish Daddy would get on home
so we can go to the show.

She sent me out to play again.
My coloring book is all filled up,
most of the crayons are broken.
I wanted to talk
about school, about how I like to read,
about how scared I am of the big boy down the block,
about what I want to be...
just talk.
Or to sit,
just sit in the same room
and watch her watch TV.

Sometimes she looks like she might say something,
then all of a sudden
the something goes away.
She looks like maybe she would talk if she knew what to say.
Dad says she doesn't know,
I know she never tried.

One day I'll be too big to send out to play.
What will she do then?

Feeling special.
What could be better
than being the one
to carry Uncle Willie's bags to the station
when his visit is through,
or trying on the new dress
Daddy brought home
just for you,
or getting the baseball cap
you always wanted
from your brother Lou.
The only thing that's better
is Mama's kiss and hug.

I don't understand
how "good" English
and five times two is ten
can help buy us more food
and extra blankets.
But Mama says it can
and she never lied to me.
So I ask my teachers,
but they don't tell.
I bet they know.
Why won't they say?

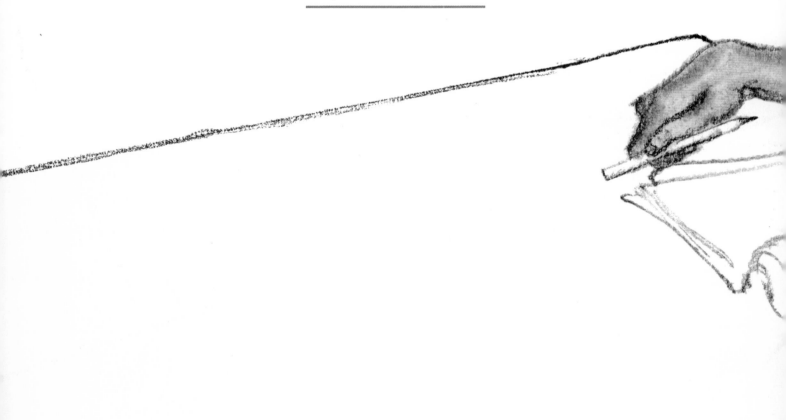

My summer vacation...
went to Jones Beach with Jo Jo's family.
Jimmy got out of jail.
I sneaked into the pool crosstown twice.
Daddy lost his second job.
Mama said don't worry,
but he did.
Sharon's sister hit the number.
That makes the fourth time.
Teacher don't want to hear that.
What can I write?
Went to Jones Beach...

Pretty.
That's what Daddy
says I am
whenever he comes
to get me.
I love him
and I'm glad
he's gonna come today.

Oh, I wish he'd hurry up!

remembering
Grandma filling up this porch
with laughing
and stories about when
Mama was a little girl
and Grandma would hug me
and say
I was her very special own granddaughter.
But now she's gone.
I miss her—

Blue.
I'm not David's girl anymore.
No more walks home from school.
No more holding hands for me.
He's with Cheryl now,
and he doesn't even care
if he broke my heart.

Tom Feelings is well known as an artist and illustrator. His books include two Caldecott Honor Books— *Moja Means One: Swahili Counting Book* and *Jambo Means Hello: Swahili Alphabet Book,* both written by Muriel Feelings and published by The Dial Press. Mr. Feelings was born in Brooklyn, New York, and attended the School of Visual Arts. He lived in West Africa for two years, and more recently in Guyana, South America, where he worked with the government publishing program, training young artists in textbook illustration. He now lives in New York City, where he is currently working on other book projects.

Nikki Grimes has already earned a reputation for her poetry, which has appeared in several magazines and anthologies, and her first novel, *Growin',* was recently published by Dial. Ms. Grimes was graduated from Livingston College, Rutgers University, in 1974. Since then she has been free-lancing as a journalist and photographer, and is currently co-producing a children's radio program on WBAI Radio in New York City.

The art in this book is reproduced in two colors: black and a warm yellow. The key plate reproduces the original drawing or painting in line or halftone, depending on the individual piece, and is printed in black ink. The second ink, either a halftone or a flat tint, enriches the black and maintains the warmth of the original art.